HER NEW HOME

Elizabeth lay on her bed like a corpse. Her long, stiff braids lay like dried cornstalks alongside her. Her face was as pale as the prairie sky. Her hair was the color of the dust that sifted in through the walls and covered everything in that Nebraska farmhouse. She looked sad and tired.

"This is Hattie," Henry said. "She reads."

"Ah," said Elizabeth. "That's good." She did not smile. It occurred to me then that she didn't know Henry was bringing home an orphan—nor did she care.

I looked about the room. There was a dresser in one corner. Near the window stood a small chair with a cane seat. Next to it was a large wooden rocker. Like mother and child, I thought, and a lump formed in my throat, so I could barely swallow. . . .

"Historical details about Nebraska farm life are engaging, and children will sympathize with Hattie and the other orphans and rejoice in the very happy ending." —*Booklist*

OTHER PUFFIN BOOKS YOU MAY ENJOY

Gratefully Yours

Jane Buchanan

PUFFIN BOOKS

PUFFIN BOOKS
Published by the Penguin Group
Penguin Putnam Books for Young Readers,
345 Hudson Street, New York, New York 10014, U.S.A.
Penguin Books Ltd, 27 Wrights Lane, London W8 5TZ, England
Penguin Books Australia Ltd, Ringwood, Victoria, Australia
Penguin Books Canada Ltd, 10 Alcorn Avenue, Toronto, Ontario, Canada M4V 3B2
Penguin Books (N.Z.) Ltd, 182-190 Wairau Road, Auckland 10, New Zealand

Penguin Books Ltd, Registered Offices: Harmondsworth, Middlesex, England

First published in the United States of America by Farrar Straus Giroux, 1997
Published by Puffin Books,
a member of Penguin Putnam Books for Young Readers, 1999

5 7 9 10 8 6

LIBRARY OF CONGRESS CATALOGING-IN-PUBLICATION DATA
Buchanan, Jane
Gratefully yours / Jane Buchanan
p cm.
Summary: In 1923, nine-year-old Hattie rides the Orphan Train from New York
to Nebraska where she must adjust to a strange new life with a farmer and
his wife, who is despondent over the loss of her two children.
ISBN 0-14-130315-8
[1. Orphans—Fiction. 2. Farm life—Nebraska—Fiction.
3. Nebraska—Fiction. 4. Death—Fiction.] I. Title.
PZ7.B82818Gr 1999
[Fic]—dc21 96-28616 CIP AC

Printed in the United States of America

To my parents
And to Ed, Mike, and Laura
Gratefully

Author's Note

*B*etween 1854 and 1929, more than 150,000 orphaned and abandoned city children rode the Orphan Trains to new lives. They were put on the trains in New York and Boston and transported to rural communities in the Midwest and elsewhere, where they were "placed out" in adoptive and foster homes.

The Orphan Train movement was started in New York City by the Reverend Charles Loring Brace, founder of the Children's Aid Society, in an attempt to deal with the city's growing population of homeless children. While a large number of those who boarded the trains acknowledged that their lives were bettered, others resented the program that placed them in uncaring and even abusive homes.

Many Orphan Train riders and their descendants spent their lives searching for their natural families. Others, content with their new lives, never felt the need. Whatever the result, the Orphan Trains are an amazing part of this nation's history. Hundreds of travelers from the later days of the Orphan Train movement are alive still, and gather periodically to share their stories.

Although this is a fictional account, the experiences of the orphans in this book are similar to those of actual Orphan Train riders. Research for this book was done with the aid of the Orphan Train Heritage Society of America in Springdale, Arkansas.

Little Orphant Annie's come to our house
   to stay,
An' wash the cups and saucers up, an' brush
   the crumbs away,
An' shoo the chickens off the porch, an'
   dust the hearth, an' sweep,
An' make the fire, an' bake the bread, an'
   earn her board-an'-keep;
An' all us other children, when the supper
   things is done,
We set around the kitchen fire an' has the
   mostest fun
A-list'nin' to the witch tales 'at Annie tells
   about,
An' the Gobble-uns 'at gits you
     Ef you
      Don't
       Watch
       Out!

     —James Whitcomb Riley
      "Little Orphant Annie" (1883)

*Gratefully
Yours*

1

My name is Hattie. When I was six years old, my mother and father and little brother, Georgie, died in a New York City tenement fire. I was the only survivor. It was 1920. There were many orphans in the city. They had places for children like us.

"Thank God," said the woman who brought me to the orphanage. She was plump, and she smiled as she took my burned and broken doll from me.

"God doesn't even know I'm alive," I told her plainly as I cast a last look at my treasured Molly.

"Child, you must not say such a thing," the woman said, stripping off my scorched pink dress and handing me a dull white one made from old sheets, which was to be my uniform at the home. "You are an orphan now. You must be grateful to those who are kind-

3

hearted enough to take you in. You must be grateful to God for sparing you."

That was the first time I was told to feel grateful. There would be many others. I did not feel grateful. I did not feel anything at all.

I stayed at the orphanage for three years. They taught me to read and write, to sew and do fine needle-work. But they did not teach me how to feel again.

When they asked me if I wanted to go on a train to find a better life, I said yes. I don't know what I expected to find at the end of the ride. But what I did find was Nebraska.

After four long days on the train, I stood with twenty-four other orphans on the platform at a train station outside of Omaha and sang a song—about gratitude. People came from towns all around to watch, some to pick an orphan of their own to take home with them, some just out of curiosity.

I wore an old, white, cotton dress, with blue flowers embroidered around the collar, and a thin gray coat. I carried a small bag, which held a change of underclothes. That was all I had to call my own.

When we finished singing, the townspeople walked around us, eyeing us up and down as though they were picking out draft horses. They poked and prodded us, feeling our muscles, checking our teeth. Would anyone want me? I wondered. Or would I be put back on the train until the next stop? I was surprised to find that I half wished I could get back on the train. At least by now the train was familiar. Not like this great emptiness of Nebraska, and these strange, prodding farmers.

"Can you read?"

The voice startled me.

"I need someone who can read."

I looked up, way up, into the pale blue eyes of the man standing next to me, and nodded. He put a big, heavy hand on my arm and took me over to Mr. Bell, the chaperon from the home.

"This one'll do," he said.

"How do you feel about that, Hattie?" Mr. Bell asked. "Do you want to go with this man?"

I did not know how to decide. One farmer looked the same as another to me, though some had children with them. He doesn't have children, I thought. Perhaps there will be enough to eat.

I nodded to Mr. Bell.

"That's fine, then," he said. "You're a lucky girl."

"God bless you," he said to Henry Jansen when they had finished signing me over. "Let us know if there are any problems." To me he added, "Write to us now and then, Hattie. Let us know how you are adjusting."

I went with Henry from the train station, leaving behind the twenty-four other orphans who had been on the train and heading to the new home miles away, which people told me I should be grateful to have.

It was a long ride by wagon to the house. The dirt road stretched ahead as far as the eye could see. Dust blew up from the dry brown fields on either side. Sometimes there were windmills. In New York City, there were no windmills. There were buildings, tall and close. And people. Lots of people. Most of them drove automobiles, although there were horses.

We did not talk on the long ride to the farm. The September wind numbed my nose and ears. Henry looked straight ahead. From time to time, he gave the reins a flick. I did not know until we arrived that Henry was bald under his brown farm hat. I saw only his thick red beard and the blond hair sticking out from under the hat, like straw.

It had been four days since I slept in a bed. Four days since I bathed. I was tired and dirty.

2

here she is," Henry said when the farm came into view at last. A large wooden house and a larger barn perched on the horizon like birds on a rooftop. A windmill rose up over them both, turning steadily.

"Who else lives there?" I asked Henry.

"Just me and Elizabeth," he said. "My wife. She's not well." Then he added, more to himself than to me, it seemed, "That's why I thought, maybe a girl . . ." His voice trailed off, and he looked sad and distant.

I wondered what she was sick with, and if it was catching. At the orphanage, when children were sick, they were quarantined so that the rest of us didn't catch whatever it was—TB oftentimes, or scarlet fever. It was frightening, too, because so many of the children came to the home after their parents died from such diseases. In the tenements, once a sickness started spreading, it swept through like fire. We knew that if children were put in quarantine, we would likely never see them again.

I felt the knot that had been gathering in my stomach all day grow a size bigger.

I looked at Henry. He was still staring straight ahead, seemingly lost in sadness. I felt awkward, and thought I ought to say something. "You must be rich," I said finally, "to have such a big house all to yourself."

Henry laughed, and I felt embarrassed.

"No," he said. "Rich we're not." And he laughed some more.

My cheeks burned. Why was he laughing? In the city, there would have been five families in a building that size. Not to mention the poor folks and orphans hiding out in the barn.

As we neared the house, two dogs came running, yapping wildly. "That'd be Jed and Old Moses," Henry said. They were big reddish-brown dogs, with long floppy ears and droopy faces. Hounds, I found out later. For hunting.

The house was gray and weathered. A fleck of paint here and there was the only sign left that it had once been white. There was a broad front porch with two weatherworn rocking chairs that tipped gently back and forth in the wind, as though occupied by ghosts. A large gray cat that Henry called Cloud lay curled on one. She looked up at me and blinked without interest.

The yard, like most of what I'd seen of Nebraska, was brown and barren. Chickens scratched, looking for food. A few orange pumpkins lay in the remains of a vegetable garden. They were the only real color I had seen since I got off the train. And even they were coated with dust scattered by the ceaseless wind.

"Drought," said Henry. "It's a wonder anything grew."

I noticed that two smaller buildings, one with a quarter moon carved into the door, stood out behind the barn. I hadn't seen them from the road.

Henry carried my bag into the house. I followed behind, slowly. I felt light-headed, and my stomach was rumbling.

The kitchen was large and cold. Dirty dishes were piled up on the counter, and the air smelled of smoke and old bacon fat.

"Fire's near out," Henry said. He took two pieces of coal out of a box in the corner and put them in the big, black, cast-iron cookstove. Sparks flew up, and bits of ash rose toward the ceiling with the gust of hot air.

"Wife ain't up to much housework," Henry said, as if to apologize for the mess. "We lost our boy in July. Measles. Girl stillborn right after. Lizzie ain't been right ever since."

So that was the sickness he had talked about. Nothing to fear, then. That kind of sickness I knew about.

"What with the farm and all," he continued, "I don't have much time for women's work."

Another reason for needing a girl, I thought. Others at the home had said that was what would happen. We weren't going to be taken in as part of a family but as free labor. I had hoped otherwise. I had so wanted to belong to somebody again. My stomach flip-flopped. If it hadn't been so empty, I might have been sick. I sat down quickly in one of the kitchen chairs.

"Water's in the basin there," he said. "It's cold, but it'll get you clean. Then I'll take you in to to meet Elizabeth."

Henry went down the dark hallway, and I could hear him talking to Elizabeth. He spoke gently, as though to a sick child.

I walked over to the washbasin. It took me a moment to realize that the ragged child I saw in the mirror was me. My chin-length black hair was windblown and tangled. My face was smudged with soot from the train. Grit had settled into my scalp and pores. My dress was wrinkled and dirty. In fact, all of me was covered with the dust that lay across Nebraska like a funeral pall.

I splashed cold water on my face and dried it with a dirt-smudged towel hanging next to the basin. There was a comb on the shelf under the mirror, and I pulled it through my hair as best I could. For once I was glad I had the short cut that had made it easier for the home to keep our hair free of bugs.

Elizabeth lay on her bed like a corpse. Her long, stiff braids lay like dried cornstalks alongside her. Her face was pale as the prairie sky. Her hair was the color of the dust that sifted in through the walls and covered everything in that Nebraska farmhouse. She looked sad and tired.

"This is Hattie," Henry said. "She reads."

"Ah," said Elizabeth. "That's good." She did not smile. It occurred to me then that she didn't know Henry was bringing home an orphan—nor did she care.

I looked about the room. There was a dresser in one corner. Near the window stood a small chair with a cane seat. Next to it was a large wooden rocker. Like mother and child, I thought, and a lump formed in my throat, so I could barely swallow.

"She's tired," Henry said. "I'll show you to the other bedrooms. They're all empty. You can choose."

I followed Henry up the dark, narrow staircase to the second floor. It was cold. The heat from the kitchen didn't reach the upstairs. There were three bedrooms off a large hallway; a fourth door led to the attic. I chose the small corner room at the end of the hall. It had a trundle bed and an oak dresser, and there was a mirror on the wall. A porcelain washbasin with a matching pitcher sat on the dresser, and a faded patchwork quilt was folded over the end of the bed. There were two windows. One looked out at the barn, the other at the brown back field divided by barbed-wire fences into squares. From that window I could see a horse nibbling on clods of dried prairie grass in the pasture.

"Sheba," said Henry. "She's Elizabeth's."

I nodded, trying to mind my manners, but suddenly feeling a need to attend to more pressing matters. "Where's the toilet?" I blurted out, embarrassed to be mentioning such a personal thing to a practical stranger.

Henry looked uncomfortable, too. His bald head

flushed red. He nodded toward the back of the house. "No indoor toilet," he said. "Privy's outside. The one with the moon on the door. The other's the smoke-house."

"Oh," I said. Then I didn't need to go so badly. It seemed a wonder that such a big house could be without a toilet. Even the home, lacking in many things, had toilets. Still, since there were never enough for all of us, we had learned to wait.

Henry shoved his hands into his pockets. "Well," he said, backing out of the room, "you put your things away and get settled. I'll start supper."

At the mention of food, my stomach rumbled again. I tried to remember the last time I'd eaten. There was breakfast on the train, but, like most of the children, I had been too nervous to eat much—unusual for me.

I put my underthings in the top drawer of the dresser. The brass pulls rattled against the empty drawers, making a hollow sound. Shivering, I sat on the bed, wrapped the quilt around me, and gazed out the window at Sheba, alone and fenced in, in the brown pasture. Before long, I fell asleep.

When I woke up, it was dark. For a while I couldn't remember where I was. I had been dreaming—hurried, chaotic dreams about the train station; about songs of gratitude; about the farmers and their wives and children, and the small, frightened-looking orphans. All the while, I could feel the rhythm of the train as it clacked endlessly along the tracks, carrying me farther and farther from everything I knew. From everything in the world, I thought as I looked out the window of the train at the vast countryside, so different from the city where I was born.

I half expected when I woke to feel the thin arm of Emily, the girl I'd shared a bed with at the home. But then I heard Henry downstairs talking to the dogs, and I remembered. I was in Nebraska, in a strange house that was full of sadness.

At last the smell of food roused me from my bed. I felt around for a switch to turn on the lights, but found none. I hadn't noticed before that there were no electric lights in the house. Even in the tenement we had lights. And toilets. Now I could no longer put off the trip to the privy. I felt my way along the dark hallway and down the stairs. A kerosene lamp offered the only light in the kitchen.

Henry was pouring steaming water from a kettle on the stove into a tub of dirty dishes in the sink. "Thought you'd never wake up," he said.

He pointed to a plate on the stove, covered with a

faded blue-checked napkin. "Kept some supper warm for you."

"I need to go . . ." I gestured to the door.

Henry nodded. He lit a candle for me. "Take a page with you," he said, pointing to an old Sears Roebuck catalogue by the door.

At first I didn't know what he meant. Then I understood. I tore off a page and went out.

It was cold and dark in the yard. I heard something howling in the distance. The candle cast shadows all around. Jed and Old Moses followed me out, sniffing at my legs. I was glad for their company. The outhouse was dark and smelly, but I was too desperate to care. Gladly, I sat over the hole in the wooden bench.

Only when I was finished did I notice the furry gray creature crouching in the corner. I thought it was the cat, Cloud, but then I noticed that it had a long, pointed nose. A rat? We'd had plenty of those in New York. I couldn't tell if it was dead or alive. I screamed and jumped up, knocking over the candle in my rush to straighten myself. The sudden blackness frightened me even more. I ran back through the dark to the house and slammed the door. Behind me I could hear the dogs take off in chase of whatever it was.

"Seen a ghost?" Henry asked. He looked as though he was trying to hide a smile.

"There was something, an animal, out there," I said. I was still breathless from running.

"Oh," said Henry. "Probably just an old possum looking for mice."

"Mice?"

He looked at me for a minute. "Not used to outdoor toilets, are you?"

I shook my head.

"Well," said Henry, "you will be."

I ate my supper in silence. The plate was heaped with food—meat, potatoes, squash, and beans.

"When you're done," Henry said, "go sit with Elizabeth. I have some chores to do in the barn." He left, and the door slammed behind him.

I ate until I felt I would burst. I thought about the meager portions of bland food we were given at the orphanage. At least here there would be enough to eat.

I washed my dishes in the tub and picked up the lamp to light my way to Elizabeth's room. I sat in the chair next to her bed. She appeared to be sleeping.

I sat for several minutes, not knowing what to do. Her face seemed so empty. It was a look I'd seen before, I realized: in my own reflection. After a while, I got up to leave.

"Henry says you read."

Her voice startled me. I nodded.

"Sit down," she said. "Read to me."

She sounded like Alice, one of the small children at the orphanage, and I felt a twinge of loneliness. I picked up the book on the bed stand and, not finding a place marker, began at the beginning.

3

I'd read half a chapter before Elizabeth fell asleep. I wasn't sure what to do then, so I just kept reading, pretending I didn't notice.

After a while Henry came in. "Here," he said, handing me a long, white nightgown. "You can sleep in this. It's Elizabeth's. It's big, but it'll keep you warm."

Upstairs, I lay in the narrow bed and shivered under the thin woolen blankets and quilt. I could see the moon through the window. It shone coldly through a cover of blue-gray clouds.

I pulled my arms close across my chest and stared at the ceiling. I listened to the house creak. I could hear the dogs pacing downstairs. Henry was speaking softly to Elizabeth in the room below me. A coal in the stove popped and crackled.

I longed for something familiar, but there was nothing. I slept fitfully. Sometime in the night I cried. When I woke, the down-filled pillow was wet and cold.

It was still dark when I heard Henry get up. The stove door squeaked open and clanged shut, and I heard the coal begin to pop and crackle. Then the kitchen door opened and banged shut, and I heard Henry's footsteps crunch on the cold, hard ground.

I got out of bed and took off my nightgown. Goose bumps sprang up on my skin. The wooden floor was like ice against my bare feet. I clambered into my dress, pulled on my woolen stockings and my shoes, and hurried to the kitchen, where the stove was doing its feeble best to take the chill out of the air.

I sat at the kitchen table and waited for Henry. He came in shortly, carrying a pail of milk and a bucket of eggs.

"Plenty of eggs for breakfast," he said. He carved a few slices off a slab of bacon. "Elizabeth likes her bacon." He looked up, pointing the knife in my direction. "You cook?" he asked.

I shook my head. At the home, we weren't allowed in the kitchen.

"We'll have to fix that," he said. "Anyway, you can peel potatoes." He gave me the potatoes and a knife, and handed me an apron to tie around my waist. "To save the peelings in," he said, "for the pigs."

I sat in the rocker by the stove, slicing off the rough, brown skins of the potatoes, collecting the peelings in the apron.

I watched Henry bring in water from the pump outside the kitchen door. He heated it on the stove and poured it into the washbasin. He washed his hands and face and the bald part of his head, which was white from lack of sun. Then he dried off with the dirty towel and buttoned up his wool shirt.

He looked at the pot of potatoes I had peeled. "That's a sorry-looking bunch of spuds," he said. He smiled, but I felt that he was mocking me. "I guess we're going to have to teach you to be a farm girl."

Embarrassed, I looked at my hands—they had small nicks in a few places where the knife had slipped—and waited for him to tell me what to do next.

Henry put the potatoes on to boil and set about making the rest of the breakfast. "You can go exploring if you like," he said.

He wants me out of his way, I thought, taking my coat from the peg on the wall and putting it on.

"I'll call you when the breakfast's ready," he added as I went out the door.

Outside, the sun had come up. The air was still cold, though, and I could see my breath. I did up the top button of my coat against the wind and walked toward the barn. The dogs followed me, sniffing at my heels. It was a relief to be out of the house, away from the eyes and ears of strangers. I wondered what I had ever thought I would find here in Nebraska. A home? Not this, surely.

The barn was dark and still. The sour smell of manure hit my nose and made it tickle. The horses were in their stalls, munching on buckets of grain. Puffs of steam came from their nostrils. Their long, black tails flicked constantly.

On the other side was a cow. I walked toward her slowly. I had seen plenty of horses in New York, pulling ice wagons through the busy streets or standing quietly in the marketplace while their owners sold wares out of carts piled high. But I'd seen cows only in pictures. She looked at me, her big brown eyes blinking. She was black-and-white, and I was surprised at how enormous she was.

The dogs sniffed around the barn, looking for something to eat. I walked closer to the cow. She stretched her neck toward me, and I put out my hand to pat her. Suddenly her long, pink tongue shot out and caught my hand in its hot, sandpapery grip. I thought she was going to swallow it. Before I could think, I hollered, "Help!" The cow let go just as suddenly, and I felt a little foolish, thinking Henry would have to come running for nothing.

But he didn't come. I could be bleeding to death down here for all he'd care, I thought.

I remembered the stories I'd heard at the orphanage: how the farmers who took us orphans in were just looking for free labor. "That's why they never send the sickly ones," a boy at the home had said. "No one wants a helpless orphan to care for." I'd thought he was just jealous. He was fifteen, too old to go on the train, and he walked with a limp. But now I was beginning to think maybe he was right.

Well, I was not helpless. I don't need Henry to come here and save me anyway, I thought. I don't need anybody.

I sat down on a stool and leaned my back against the barn wall. Cloud came over and sniffed my legs. She rubbed against them, purring. I sat still, and she jumped up and curled into a ball on my lap. I reached my fingers into her soft gray fur. They tingled with warmth. And somewhere inside me, a memory tingled, too.

Tears prickled in my eyes. I shook my head to clear

the thoughts away. I'd learned long ago that it did no good to think about my life before. I stood up briskly, and the cat leaped to the ground. The tingling stopped, but my lap, where Cloud had lain, felt cold and empty.

4

S**ee you met the cow," Henry said when I went back to the house. I wondered how he knew that was why I yelled.

"She tried to bite me," I said.

"No," Henry said. The corner of his mouth twitched. Did he think it was funny? "Not Josephine. Gentle as a kitten. She was just being friendly. Always a surprise for the young ones, though, first time she gives them a kiss."

A kiss? She tried to swallow me whole. I could not see anything amusing about it. I felt humiliated.

"Never mind," Henry said. "You're all in one piece now." He looked me up and down. "S'pose we'll have to get you some new clothes," he said. "That old frock isn't going to last you long out here, God knows. And you'll need a warm overcoat. Gets cold out here in a hurry."

Did he think it didn't get cold in New York? I looked down at my dress. The trip to the barn hadn't improved it any. It would be nice to have some new clothes. It had been a long time.

"We'll go into town this morning. Meantime, you eat your breakfast and go on and tend to Elizabeth while I get some chores done."

Elizabeth was sitting up in bed, gazing blankly out the window, when I went in. Her breakfast, half-eaten, was on the nightstand, next to some vials of medicine—for her sickness, Henry had explained. The food was cold, and the fat from the bacon had hardened in a greasy white pool on her plate.

I stood for a moment, waiting for her to notice me. When she didn't, I gathered my courage and said, "Good morning."

She turned her head slowly and looked at me as though she had never seen me before. She shifted her gaze back to the window.

Not knowing what else to do, I went to the dresser and picked up her brush. It was beautiful: silver, set with boar's bristles, and there was a matching silver comb with tortoiseshell teeth. I longed for hair to my knees so I could run that brush through it and make it shine.

I took the brush over to the bed and sat next to Elizabeth. She was still as I untied the ribbons at the ends of her braids and gently untwisted the hair, forming long golden ringlets. I began to brush them out, starting from the bottom and working my way to the top.

She seemed so fragile to me. Breakable as a china doll. I had never known a grown person who was so helpless. I thought, She is as lonely as I am. She is as empty as I.

With the comb, I divided her hair into two parts, then each part into three, and braided it again, fastening it at the ends with carefully tied bows of white ribbon.

Then, because I could think of nothing else to do, I picked up her breakfast plate and carried it out to the kitchen, where Henry was waiting, drinking coffee out of a blue enamel cup.

"Will she be all right here alone?" I asked him.

"Can't be helped," he said. "Used to have my relatives over to look after her, but she doesn't tolerate them much these days. Besides, they've got their own to take care of. Elizabeth's family's back East, and Ma doesn't travel much." He looked sadly down the hallway and sighed. "She'll likely sleep while we're gone," he said.

He picked up a basket of fresh brown eggs. "For trading at the dry goods store," he said.

Henry brought the wagon around, and I climbed in, curious to take my first trip to town. I imagined myself in a pretty new dress. One that had been bought just for me, and wasn't already worn at the elbows and frayed in the hem. Perhaps the boy at the home was wrong, I thought. Perhaps Henry did want a daughter, and not a servant.

As we drove along the bumpy dirt road, I watched while mile after mile of dry brown earth passed by, with an occasional patch of sunburnt grass thrown in. Now and then there was a farmhouse. Fences divided up the emptiness, and windmills rose into the sky, turning endlessly. From time to time, Henry pointed out a bird overhead, or sitting on a wire, and told me its name. I was surprised that someone so big would take notice of something so small.

Occasionally we came upon another wagon, or even an automobile on the road, and we had to breathe the dust it kicked up behind it. But mostly the road was deserted.

Town was a row of two- and three-story brick buildings on each side of the wide main street. Wagons were hitched up alongside automobiles in the middle of the street.

Henry tethered the horses, and we walked over to the dry goods store. On the way, we passed a photography studio. Through the window I could see a couple and their daughter posing for a portrait. The girl was wearing a pale blue dress with a low waist and tiny pearl buttons, and shiny black shoes with T-straps across the instep instead of high-buttoned shoes. Her yellow hair was done up in curls and blue ribbons. The mother was sitting next to her on a high-backed chair, and she was smiling at the girl. The father, behind them both, was resting his hands gently on their shoulders. He was smiling, too. I wondered if that girl knew how lucky she was.

Next to the photography shop was a bakery. The window was filled with cakes and breads and cinnamon rolls. The smell made my mouth water. I wanted to ask Henry to stop so I could look some more, but I held my tongue.

The next store was Bascomb's Dry Goods. The worn wooden floors creaked as we walked in. The small, white-haired man behind the counter knew Henry.

"How are you today, Mr. Bascomb?" Henry said.

"Nice day, Henry," Mr. Bascomb said. "Who've we got here?" He looked at me.

"This is Hattie. She's staying with us."

"One of them orphans, is she?"

Henry nodded.

"Well, young lady," Mr. Bascomb said, "you're lucky to be staying with the Jansens. They're good folks. I've known Henry here all his life. Lord knows, he can use the help."

I felt my face redden. The help. When I didn't answer, Mr. Bascomb looked embarrassed. He cleared his throat and spoke to Henry. "Well then," he said, "what can I do for you, Henry?"

Henry gave Mr. Bascomb a list and the basket of eggs, and I looked around the store. There were dresses of all colors. I imagined myself in a pale blue one with a low waist and tiny pearl buttons up the front. I would wear it with white silk stockings and a pair of black T-strap shoes like the ones the girl in the photography shop was wearing.

Henry was taking a long time talking to Mr. Bascomb, so I looked around some more. On a shelf on the other side of the store was a display of china dolls of all descriptions. One of them, a girl doll with long black hair done up in ringlets, caught my eye. She was smiling, and there were dimples in her pink cheeks. I wished I could take her home and have tea parties with her. And at night in my bed, I could hold her tight when I woke in the dark. I would call her Molly.

"Bit old for dolls, aren't you?" Henry's voice startled me.

I nodded, taking one last look at the doll.

"Well," he said, "better move along if we're going to be getting you some clothes."

I looked at the racks of clothes on display. "But—"

"They've got a box over at the church," Henry said. "We ought to be able to find you something there."

The charity box. I should have known. Why would he buy me a pale blue dress with pearl buttons? I wasn't his daughter, after all. I was only an orphan.

5

The church stood alone at the edge of town in a patch of dead grass. It was wooden and plain and painted white. Not like the fancy carved stone building with stained-glass windows we had gone to in New York.

When the wagon drove up, a small man dressed in black came running out to greet us.

"Henry!" he said, clasping Henry's hands. "How are you? How is Elizabeth? I've meant to get out to see her. And who is this poor child? I heard you'd taken in one of those little orphans." He was speaking fast, as if he was nervous.

"This is Hattie, Pastor Schiller," Henry said. "She needs some clothes."

"Why, of course. Yes, come right in. We'll fix her up."

I followed them up the front steps into the church.

The charity box was in the back room. Henry and Pastor Schiller picked out a few things and held them up to me to see how they would fit.

"These ought to do," Henry said, collecting a bundle of dull dresses, a brown woolen coat, and a pair of worn, black high-buttoned shoes.

"Yes," said Pastor Schiller. "We're lucky to have such generous parishioners to help out those less fortunate than ourselves." He smiled at me and patted my head. I didn't smile back.

"Better be going, then," Henry said. "Don't like to leave Elizabeth too long."

"Of course," said Pastor Schiller. "I'll be coming out to see her." From the way he said it, I didn't expect we'd be seeing him at the farm anytime soon. "And we'll be looking forward to seeing you in church on Sunday, Hattie," he said, turning to me. "We'll be welcoming all our orphans."

He was trying to be kind, I supposed, but his words stung. "Our orphans." But at least now I knew others from the home had been placed out here. I wondered who.

Henry put the clothes in the back of the wagon. "They're clean, anyway," he said. "They'll do for farm work."

I glared at him. Sure, I thought, they're just fine for all our poor little orphans. I imagined the dresses I would have worn if my parents had been alive, if I were not an orphan, if somebody loved me. Then I would have a pale blue dress with pearl buttons.

It was afternoon when we got back to the house. Elizabeth was in the kitchen, in her dressing gown, stirring something on the stove.

"It's good to see you up and about," Henry said softly.

Elizabeth looked at him, then back to the pot. "Somebody needed to make supper," she said dully.

Henry peered into the pot. "Good day for chicken stew," he said. "Hattie." He turned to me. "You go put on one of them clean dresses and help Elizabeth with supper."

As I started up to my room, I could hear Elizabeth say to Henry, "We can't be affording to buy clothes."

"It's all right," I heard Henry say. "They're from the church."

"I'll not be beholden to that place," Elizabeth said. She sounded angry.

There was a pause. "Pastor Schiller asked for you," Henry said.

"Pastor Schiller." Elizabeth almost spit the name. "He can ask for me till hell freezes if he thinks I'll set foot—"

"We promised to take the girl to church," Henry said.

"You promised," Elizabeth said. "I never said I wanted the girl here."

Henry quieted her then. And I went on up the stairs, my cheeks burning with shame and hurt.

Cloud was asleep on the bed. I shooed her off and sat down. She rubbed against my ankles for a moment, then flicked her tail at me and left. Outside my window, I could see Sheba standing alone in the pasture. I knew just how she felt. "She doesn't want you either, does she, girl?" I said.

I put on one of the dresses. It was brown with small pink flowers, dulled from washing. It was too big, just as everything at the home had been. "It'll last longer if she has room to grow," they always said. The shoes were too big, too, and the toes slapped the floor when I walked. I looked in the mirror and tried to straighten my hair, which seemed to get wilder with each day. My face was streaked with dust again, from the ride to town. Looking at myself, I had a vague memory of a pink dress, and a girl with glistening black curls. I shook away the thought, washed my face with the cold water in the basin on the dresser. I went down-stairs, my new shoes slapping each step.

"That's a sight better," said Henry when I walked into the kitchen. "Plenty of room for a growing girl, too," he added.

Elizabeth looked up from her cooking. She flicked a braid over her shoulder and went back to stirring. "Supper's ready," she said.

I wanted to yell at her. I wanted to say, It's not my fault your children are dead. But I said nothing, just took my place at the table.

Supper was quiet. Elizabeth didn't look up from her plate. But the food was delicious—thick chicken stew, biscuits dripping with butter. Even when my stomach ached from eating, I wanted more.

I washed the dishes and put them to dry while Henry helped Elizabeth back to bed. Later, when I went in to read, as Henry directed, I tried to remember that Elizabeth was sick. But it didn't ease the hurt.

Finally, after Elizabeth fell asleep, Henry came in. "Best be turning in," he said. "Tomorrow you start learning to be a farm girl."

6

That night I woke to feel something heavy on my feet. It was warm, and I thought maybe Henry had brought me an extra blanket. But when I moved my feet, it moved, too. It was Cloud. I pushed her off the bed with my foot and turned over. A minute later, she was back. I lay still, and she snuggled back down at my feet.

By morning she had moved all the way up to the head of the bed, and when I opened my eyes, I had a face full of fur. I lay in bed, with Cloud purring softly beside me, and listened to the morning sounds—the coal crackling, Henry going in and out, a rooster crowing.

"Today I learn to be a farm girl," I said to Cloud. She looked up at me and blinked. I blinked back and sighed. "Guess there's no use putting it off."

I climbed out of my warm bed and hurried into the

cold dress that was hanging from a peg on the wall. I put on my big, floppy shoes and slapped down the stairs.

Henry had already made a big batch of griddle cakes. "Eat up," he said. "We've got a lot to do today."

I looked down the hall at Elizabeth's room, wondering if she was coming to breakfast. Henry saw me.

"She's not feeling well this morning," he said. "I'll keep something warm for her."

It seemed strange that some days Elizabeth could be up and about, and other days she could hardly rouse herself. But after yesterday, I was glad she would be in bed today.

"There, now," Henry said, putting down a plate of griddle cakes drowning in molasses, with bacon and sour pickles. "Eat up so we can get to those chores." I nodded and dug in despite myself.

The strong smell of manure hit my nose as I walked into the barn. It made my eyes water. I wondered if I would ever get used to it.

I stayed clear of Josephine, even though Henry swore she was gentle.

"Josie likes you," said Henry.

"She tried to bite me," I said, remembering the sandpapery tongue wrapped around my hand.

"Naw," said Henry. "That's just her way of saying hello. Haven't you ever heard of a cowlick?"

I looked at Josie. She winked her big brown eye. "What does she know anyway?" I said. "She's just a dumb animal."

"Josie?" Henry said, rubbing the cow's nose. "She knows more about love than most people. All animals do. It's instinct."

Josephine winked again. I slowly reached out and patted her nose. It was warm on my cold hand, and softer than I thought it would be.

"Soon I'll teach you to milk her," Henry said.

That'll be the day, I thought, but I didn't say so.

At the other end of the barn were the sheep. Six ewes, five white and one black.

"What's that one's name?" I asked, pointing to the black one.

"Doesn't have one."

"How come she's black?"

"All the others I raised myself. That one was a gift from the neighbors."

Neighbors. I thought about the fields spread out on all sides and wondered where there could ever be neighbors.

We had to go outside again to get to the chicken

coop. The sun was hanging just over the edge of the earth, like an egg yolk. The fresh air smelled good after the stuffiness of the barn. I gulped it in hungrily.

"This'll be your job," said Henry, "feeding the chickens and gathering the eggs every morning before breakfast."

The chickens were scratching around, pecking at the dusty ground, cocking their heads from side to side. They were all sizes and colors. A tall, brown rooster, biggest in the flock, stood guard.

"Watch out for him," Henry said. "He's a mean one."

I wondered how a chicken could be mean. "Don't chickens have instincts?" I asked.

"They may be the exception," Henry said with a chuckle. "Plain stupid creatures they are."

Henry showed me how to spread the corn for the chickens to eat. After they squawked off looking for breakfast, we picked up the eggs one by one from the nests and placed them carefully in the tin pail. They were warm on my bare fingers. I could see what Henry meant about chickens being stupid: didn't they wonder where their eggs went while they were off scratching for corn?

When we were done with the chickens, Henry took me to see the pigs. Even outside, the pigsty smelled terrible. I held my nose. The pigs looked up and grunted, then went back to rooting for their breakfast. They were kind of cute, as long as you didn't breathe.

"Don't like the smell?" Henry asked. I shook my head. "Well," he said, "just remember, that's where that bacon you ate this morning came from."

I glanced back at the pigs. It was hard to imagine them as breakfast.

"We'll be slaughtering them before winter," Henry said matter-of-factly. "Some we'll sell. Some we'll eat. That's life on a farm."

And death, I thought, with a twinge of sympathy for the pigs. I wondered how Henry could bring himself to kill them.

When it was time to go back to the house, I was kind of sorry. Henry was different in the barn. It was as if the memories in the house, and Elizabeth's illness, were weights he shed when he was out of doors.

7

It was still dark when I woke up early the next morning. I got dressed, then picked up Cloud and went downstairs. I wondered whether Elizabeth would be getting out of bed today. Henry looked up when I walked in.

"Best get your chores done. Then wash yourself and put on your Sunday finest," he said. "Church today."

Sunday. I'd lost track of the days. As I grabbed the pail and made my way out to the chicken coop, I wondered which of the old dresses from the charity box Henry thought was fine. I wondered if Elizabeth would be coming with us.

The chickens began to squawk when they saw me. I spread the corn the way Henry had showed me, and gathered the eggs from the abandoned nests. I watched the roosters strutting around the yard, pecking at corn, their colorful tail feathers glinting in the early rays of sunshine. Then I walked back to the house, hungry for breakfast.

I'd barely finished eating when Elizabeth came out of her room dressed in a blue churchgoing dress, her hair all done up at the back of her head. It was as if she had never said that about hell freezing. She put me in a washtub full of hot water and scrubbed my hair so hard I thought it would be a miracle if I had any left when she was done. I was surprised at how strong she was.

She combed the knots out of my hair and took to clipping it all around. When she was finished, I thought I looked almost like one of those ladies pictured in the Sears Roebuck catalogue.

She had me bring down the charity dresses and picked out the least ragged of them, a green one with a high collar and long sleeves. I put it on, and she pinned and snipped and tucked it until it didn't look half bad. She tied a pink satin ribbon in my hair, and another around my waist, and put some blacking on my shoes. When I caught a glimpse of myself in Elizabeth's mirror, I could hardly believe it was me. I looked almost pretty. I felt warm all over to think Elizabeth was taking such time to make me look wanted. I turned to thank her, but she looked at me with blank eyes and said, "I won't have people saying I don't know how to care for a child," and walked away.

I sat down hard on the bed, as though I'd been kicked by a horse. My eyes stung. I hate her, I thought, holding my fists tight in my lap. I hate it here. I wish I had never gotten on that train. I wish Mr. Bell would come and take me back.

On the way to church, I sat wedged between Henry and Elizabeth in the wagon, a blanket over our laps. Nobody spoke, and I leaned over to Henry's side so that I wouldn't have to touch Elizabeth, which seemed to be fine with her because she didn't so much as look at me.

The church bell was ringing when we arrived. There were automobiles, carriages, and wagons parked around the building. Parishioners were milling about, greeting one another before going in.

"Hattie! Hattie!"

I turned at the sound of a familiar voice. It was Emily. I got a lump in my throat just seeing her. A familiar face. With being so angry at Elizabeth, I'd all but forgotten that Pastor Schiller said there would be other orphans here.

"Oh, Hattie!" she cried. "You look beautiful. I hardly knew you. How are you doing? Is this your family? No other children? I have so many, I still can't remember all their names—"

"Whoa!" said Henry, holding up his hands. "Slow down, miss." His eyes were fairly twinkling. "You going to introduce us to this young lady, Hattie?"

"This is Emily," I said. "We shared a room at the orphanage."

"A room?" Emily said. "A bed, more like. Everybody had to share, didn't we, Hattie?"

I looked at Emily as she rattled on in that excited way she had. She was wearing the same dress she'd worn on the train, I realized. Not even charity-box clothes for her. But, despite her worn clothing, she was a pretty girl. Her blond hair and blue eyes had always made me feel so plain. She looked, I realized suddenly, as if she belonged with Henry and Elizabeth. And the way Henry was looking at her, it seemed that he would have liked it that way. I wondered if he was wishing he'd seen her first at the train depot.

"And Peter and Hank," Emily continued, "are with a family outside town. Peter says he hates it and is going to run away. I think he should give it more of a try, don't you? David went to a judge's house. He lives in a big white house right in the city. The only child, can you imagine?"

I wondered how she knew all this. But Emily always did have a way of finding things out.

A woman carrying two babies and surrounded by children looked angrily across the way at Emily. "Maryann!" she called. "Come along."

I gave Emily a questioning look. She shrugged, but her cheeks were red. "She already had an Emily," she said.

The woman had reached us by then.

"Morning, Mrs. Dewhurst," Henry said, tipping his hat.

Mrs. Dewhurst nodded her head in Henry's direction. Then she shoved a baby at Emily and took her by the arm. "Come along," she said, leading Emily away. "You're supposed to be looking after the children, not standing around gabbing."

"That woman has too many children." Henry shook his head. "Like the old woman who lived in a shoe."

I watched Emily being led roughly away. Then I looked up at Elizabeth's empty face. Suddenly she didn't seem quite so bad.

8

*W*e sat near the back of the church. From there I could see most everyone. I picked out several orphans who'd been placed out here. Besides Emily and me, there were the brothers Peter and Hank, sitting slouched down in their seats next to a tall, heavyset man with a scowl on his face, and his thin, palefaced wife. While I watched, the man, who was even bigger than Henry, took a hand to the back of Peter's head and barked at him to sit up straight. I jumped as if it were me he had hit. Why did people have to be so hateful? They'd told us before we even left New York that brothers and sisters shouldn't count on being able to stay together, so I guess Peter and Hank were lucky that way. At least they had each other.

David was sitting right up front with a proud-looking man dressed in a fine black suit. No feeding chickens for him, I thought. He'd always gotten teased by the boys for his carrot hair and freckles. I guessed no one would be laughing at him now.

Michael, another child from the orphanage, was sitting with a little boy. Emily hadn't mentioned that he was here. He and the boy were talking and laughing. A smiling man and woman were sitting with them, trying to get them to be still.

And little Alice, with her long pigtails brushed to shining, was perched in the lap of a plump, rosy-cheeked woman with five children who looked just like her. I never did figure out how Alice got to keep those pigtails when the rest of us had ours cut short. But she was so sweet-natured, she'd always been a favorite of the ladies at the home.

I didn't see any of the others. Perhaps they had been placed in nearby towns, or maybe they'd gotten back on the train to try again at the next stop.

After a while the organist began to play and everyone quieted down. Pastor Schiller got up and read from the Bible. He talked about charity and the "poor unfortunate orphans" who had joined the flock. I thought about the black sheep in Henry's barn. He went on and worked himself into a sweat talking about the filth and vice of the cities and how the good-hearted, clean-living farmers were going to save the country. He talked about God preserving us from lives of sin. He talked about gratitude.

I looked at Emily. What had she to be grateful for? What had I?

After the service, on the way out, Pastor Schiller took Elizabeth's hand and smiled. "How good to see you again, Elizabeth," he said.

She just stood straight and looked him in the eye and took back her hand. It was the same cold gaze I'd felt on me that morning, and I almost pitied Pastor Schiller.

"We brought the girl," she said, "because Henry promised them we would. That's all."

Pastor Schiller stopped smiling, then looked at me. "My," he said, and he smiled again, "don't we look pretty?" He chanced another smile at Elizabeth. "You did a fine job with those clothes," he said.

Elizabeth straightened a bit more, if that was possible. She almost looked pleased.

As we filed out of the church, I noticed Emily, trying to carry a baby and dragging a little boy along behind her. When she saw me, she stopped for a moment and smiled.

"Maryann, don't dawdle," Mrs. Dewhurst snapped. Emily shrugged again and moved on.

I wanted to cry. Poor Emily. First she had lost her

family. Now she didn't even have her name. I climbed into the wagon next to Henry. "It just isn't fair," I said.

Henry looked at me. "Who ever said life was fair?" He gave the reins a flick, and the horses moved forward with a jerk.

9

Sunday dinner was pot roast with vegetables and gravy. But it seemed tasteless, and left me feeling empty. I kept thinking about what Henry said, about life not being fair. It just wasn't right that some people should be placed out with judges and others with the likes of Mrs. Dewhurst. It wasn't as if we had a choice, not really. Mr. Bell had asked me whether I wanted to go on the train, even whether I wanted to go with Henry. But if I had said no, then what? It might have been better, but after today I could see that it might have been much worse.

When we finished eating, Elizabeth started the dishes. I was surprised. You never knew with her. It must be hard on Henry, I thought, never knowing what to expect.

When the dishes were dried and put away, we all retired to the sitting room. It was the Lord's day, and though Elizabeth didn't seem to have much use for church, she still appeared to hold Sundays sacred. There would be no work today.

She sat by the fire and read to herself for a change, the poems of Ralph Waldo Emerson. Henry took his place at the big oak desk in the corner of the room and began reading the *Farm Journal*. I sat down, too, feeling awkward. Was I to sit and watch?

Finally, as though he'd just remembered I was there, Henry said, "You ought to go up to the attic, Hattie, and find a book for yourself."

I looked at him, surprised.

"Sure," Henry said. "There's piles of them up there, aren't there, Lizzie?"

Elizabeth raised her head and smiled vaguely.

"Elizabeth wasn't always a farmer's wife, you know. She used to be a schoolteacher."

I looked at Elizabeth, who appeared almost ghostly in the flickering firelight. It didn't seem possible that she had once commanded a classroom. Although when I thought about the force of her anger toward Pastor Schiller, I guessed maybe she could have. Then, remembering her coldness toward me that morning, I decided she was probably a mean, spiteful teacher who rapped her pupils' knuckles with a ruler at the slightest misconduct.

"Go take a look," Henry said. "Top of the stairs, last door to the left. Take a lamp. It's dark up there."

The wood creaked as I climbed the narrow staircase to the attic. Henry was right. It was dark. And cold. There was the smell of old things shut away. I rubbed my hands together for warmth. It took a while for my eyes to become adjusted to the dim light, even with the lamp. But after a while I could make out the shapes of the items piled there. Some, I supposed, had been there for ages. Others, like the small wooden cradle and rocking horse, were probably more recent additions.

There were trunks, too. And bandboxes of all shapes and sizes, covered in wallpapers of different designs. Odd pieces of furniture lined the walls. There was a small oak secretary, with bookshelves and a fold-down desktop, and lots of little pigeonholes for putting things in. Elizabeth's? I wondered. Old chairs with seats missing sat waiting to be repaired.

A small wooden table stood near the middle of the room with a stack of photographs facedown on top of it. I turned one over. It was a photograph of a man and a woman with a small child. Henry with more hair, I realized, and Elizabeth looking young and happy with her son on her lap. Then there was love in her eyes. I felt my cheeks redden, as if I had walked in on a private moment. Quickly I turned the picture over and looked around for the books.

I spotted them in a far corner, stacked neatly against the wall with their titles facing out. I didn't know much about books, although I was a capable reader. But I'd found myself held in rapture by the book I was reading to Elizabeth, in spite of the awkwardness I felt when I was with her. I wondered whether these books could be as good.

I decided to take the top book from the first pile and work my way down. *The Wonderful Wizard of Oz* by L. Frank Baum.

I picked up the lamp and went back down the staircase, closing the door behind me. My dress was covered with dust. I brushed it off, sneezing from the small dust cloud I'd created.

When I got back downstairs, I found that Elizabeth had gone to bed. "For a nap," Henry said, and he went back to reading his journal.

I was just as glad. I was getting used to Henry, but Elizabeth made me nervous. I sat in the rocking chair and opened the book. My fingers were still cold from the attic, and I found it difficult to turn the pages. But they warmed up as the heat from the fire reached them. Cloud jumped up into my lap and curled into a ball. Soon she was asleep and purring, and I was on my way to Oz.

10

I had no idea how long I'd been asleep in my chair when Henry woke me to tell me it was bedtime. There was moonlight shining through the window.

"Best be getting to bed," he said. "Tomorrow you learn to ride."

"Ride?"

He nodded. "Farm girl's got to know how to handle a horse," he said.

"A horse?" I must have sounded ridiculous, but I supposed it had to do with being awakened from a sound sleep with dreams of wicked witches, and trying to understand what Henry was talking about.

That night I dreamed about flying to Oz on a winged horse, with my cat, Toto, asleep in my lap. Elizabeth was chasing after me, saying, "I never wanted her," over and over, and cackling like a witch. I woke up in a cold sweat and lay in bed listening to my heartbeat.

I lay there for a while before I folded the covers aside and sat up. Cloud stretched and yawned. She looked annoyed at having to move from the warm bed.

"We might as well get up as lie here staring at the ceiling," I said. I got dressed and went downstairs. There was no sign of Henry, and the stove was nearly out. I put on my coat and picked up the pail and headed to the barn.

It was dark and cold outside, and the sky was clear. The chickens were already up and clucking. I spread the corn and carefully gathered the eggs. When I took them into the kitchen, Henry was there, clearly surprised to see me.

"Didn't hear you get up!" he said.

"I couldn't sleep," I said. I didn't mention the dream.

After breakfast, Henry pushed his chair back from the table. "Well," he said, "guess we'd better get out to the barn. Those horses need their exercise."

He took me to the barn, where Sheba was waiting, and strapped on her saddle.

"Up you go," he said.

I looked at Henry, and I looked at the horse. My head was barely as high as her back.

Henry looked as if he was trying not to laugh. "Here," he said, "put your foot in the stirrup and I'll give you a boost."

I had to stretch to reach the stirrup, but with Henry's help I pulled myself up. I held on to the saddle horn for dear life. I'd never been up so high. With a jolt that nearly sent me toppling, Sheba began to walk, while Henry held the reins. After a bit I relaxed, and the knot in my stomach unwound. I even enjoyed the feeling of being up so high with the prairie wind blowing through my hair. Like a cowboy, I thought. I laughed an old, rusty laugh that caused Henry to look at me in surprise.

"Feels good, don't it?"

I nodded.

"Here, take the reins."

I shook my head, sure that if I let go of the saddle horn, I would fall.

"Go ahead," he said. "Sheba's a good horse."

"I know," I said, remembering what he'd said about Josephine, "gentle as a kitten."

"That's right." Henry nodded. "And she's got good instincts."

Sheba seemed to know just what to do. She walked slow and steady, and turned easy when I pulled the reins. Henry went back to the barn and saddled up his horse. "I been meaning to check the fences out in the back," he said. "Want to come along?"

I nodded, and Sheba turned and followed Henry out to the pasture. We rode over a swell in the land, and there was a small apple grove and cow pond with a windmill beside it for pumping water. A little broken-down shack stood nearby, built into the side of the hill. It had no windows and no roof. Cloud was sunning herself in the doorway. She stood up and stretched when she saw us.

"The old homesteading cabin," Henry said. "My pa built it when he and Ma first came to Nebraska. Half sod it was, half wood. I was born here. Haven't been able to think about tearing it down." He paused. "Guess nature'll do it for me before much longer."

We stopped there, looking for a while. Then Henry said, "Use a rest?"

My arms and shoulders were tired from all the riding, and I had blisters on my hands. I nodded.

Henry dismounted and helped me down. It felt strange to be on solid ground again. My legs were wobbly.

I sat in the doorway of the cabin with Cloud in my

lap while Henry walked around, checking the fences and the windmill. "When it freezes," he said, "we'll come down and cut ice for the icehouse." He scowled a bit. "Pond's usually deeper. But this drought . . . Lucky we have anything." He looked at the sky, pale and gray. "Maybe if we get a good winter," he said.

We started back to the house. Cloud bounded off after a field mouse. Henry shook his head as he watched her. "She's supposed to be catching mice in the barn so they won't eat the grain. Useless old cat." But he smiled, and I knew he didn't mean it.

After that I took Sheba out every day, first with Henry, and then on my own. I stopped being sore all over, and the blisters on my hands turned to calluses.

When I was done with my chores, and if Elizabeth and Henry didn't need me, I'd take a book and ride out to the old cabin. I'd sit in the doorway with Cloud in my lap, and read until my hands got too cold or my stomach too empty.

I discovered that the attic was a treasure chest of stories. When I finished *The Wonderful Wizard of Oz*, I moved on to *Alice's Adventures in Wonderland*, and then to *The Wind in the Willows*. I would sit and imagine Toad, Ratty, and Mole living on the banks of the cow pond.

I could put the rest of the world out of my mind. Between hard work and reading, I had little time to think about the future.

But that wouldn't last. One day near the middle of October, Henry came to the barn, where I was brushing down Sheba, and said, "Monday you'll take her to school."

School. It had been part of the agreement. I was to go to church and school. Most of the others from the train had already started, I knew from Emily. She always rattled on about it at church.

"Why aren't you in school?" she'd asked one Sunday.

"Elizabeth needs someone," I said. "Henry doesn't like to leave her alone. And he's getting the farm ready for winter."

But now the work was done. The corn was in the crib, the hayloft full. The root cellar was stocked, and the buildings repaired. Henry and a neighbor, Mr. Schmidt, had spent a week slaughtering pigs and hanging the carcasses in the smokehouse. The smell of hickory smoke was thick in the air. Henry and Mr. Schmidt always helped each other out this time of year, Henry said. Neither of them could afford to hire hands, but there were some things a man just couldn't do alone. Henry gave Mr. Schmidt some of his hams in payment, and Mr. Schmidt gave Henry beef.

I had stayed as far away as I could while the slaughtering was being done, but still I could hear the squeals of the pigs. Now when I went out to do my chores, I avoided the empty pigpen. But with all that over, Henry could stay close to the house. Close to Elizabeth. And I could go to school.

The school year had begun weeks ago. I would be the new girl. I knew from experience at the home that being new was among the greatest sins a person could commit. There would be a price to pay. And if being new wasn't bad enough, being the new orphan would be even worse.

I sat down on a stool in the stable. Cloud jumped up in my lap and began to knead with her paws, as if I were a lump of bread dough.

"I'll be all right, Cloud," I said, more to myself than to her. "It's only school. I'll be back every night. And I'll be able to see more of Emily and the others."

11

❧

The Disappointment Creek School was a small, wooden structure with a bell tower on top. It looked, like the farm, as if it had once been painted white. It stood next to a hollow where the creek ran until it dried up, causing the homesteaders great disappointment and giving them something to name their school after.

Behind the school there were outhouses, one for girls and one for boys. The coal shed was in between so the boys couldn't peek through the knotholes at the girls. The school yard was dirt, trampled hard as stone. Not a stalk of prairie grass could take root in it.

It was a warm day for the season. As Henry and I rode up, twenty or so children in the yard looked at us in wonderment. Hadn't they ever seen horses before? Most of the twenty were barefoot.

I tied Sheba to a hitching post and followed Henry into the school. Inside, there was only one room. Benches and desks were arranged in rows around a small potbellied stove. The teacher's desk was at the front, with painted pine boards serving as a blackboard behind it. Pictures of George Washington and Abraham Lincoln looked down from the wall over the blackboard, and an American flag hung from a pole at one end.

Henry introduced me to the teacher, Mr. Givens. "She reads," he said, "and ciphers."

"Well, that's fine," Mr. Givens said. "Most of our orphans are poor readers." He smiled, showing big white teeth.

Mr. Givens was tall and dark-haired, with a bushy mustache curled at the ends. His skin was pale. I guessed he didn't spend much time outdoors. He wore a black suit and vest, a white shirt, and a thin black necktie.

"You may take a seat in the fourth row, Hattie," Mr. Givens said. "I'll be calling the others in."

I sat down on the bench at the end of the row. The school bell clanged loudly overhead. I could hear the students lining up outside the door. When they were quiet, Mr. Givens led them in. The youngest children sat in the front three rows, and the oldest boys and girls were in the back. The third class, the one I was in, took up the middle.

A red-haired boy sat down next to me, and I felt an elbow jab hard into my side. "Stole my seat, orphan," the boy said through his teeth. "My daddy says you orphans are always stealing. That's why your parents sent you away."

I clutched my side and stared hard at the desk. The names and pictures carved in the top were blurred by the tears in my eyes. I bit my lip to keep from crying out loud.

"Children," Mr. Givens said, "we have another new pupil today. Hattie will be in the third class for the time being. She's also one of our orphan children. I trust you will make her feel welcome."

I heard a giggle behind me. "Did you have something to say, Joseph?" Mr. Givens asked sternly.

"I said, 'Little Orphant Annie,' " Joseph said. Titters broke out all over the classroom.

"Your interest in poetry is commendable, Joseph," Mr. Givens said. "Perhaps you can memorize Mr. Riley's poem and recite it in class tomorrow morning."

Joseph groaned.

"Now, all rise for the Pledge of Allegiance."

I tried not to look at the red-haired boy. Instead I

glanced around the room, trying to find familiar faces.

I saw Hank across the aisle, but not Peter. I wondered if he really had run away. Michael was up front next to the little boy I had seen him with in church. David was not there. Emily had said he'd gone to a school for rich boys somewhere. And there was Emily in the third row. She looked tired and ragged. But she saw me looking at her, and she smiled.

After the pledge there was the Lord's Prayer, and then the Bible lesson. We older children worked on spelling while the little ones did their recitations with Mr. Givens. I finished early and was listening to Michael recite his lesson when the red-haired boy jabbed me in the ribs again.

"Trying to show off how smart you are, orphan? Won't make any difference. You still ain't got no mama."

My ears were burning. I bent my head down, and that was when I noticed that the red-haired boy was barefoot. Before I could stop myself, I brought my heel down on his littlest toe. Did he ever holler!

"What's going on here?" Mr. Givens demanded.

"She stepped on my toe," the boy wailed.

"Is that true, Hattie?"

I nodded.

"Why did you step on Matthew's toe?"

I shrugged. I did not want to repeat what Matthew had said.

"Come up here, Hattie, and stand in the corner. I will have to send home a note. This is no way to begin your scholarship at Disappointment Creek."

12

❦

At midmorning Mr. Givens let us out for a break. Boys and girls lined up at the outhouses. I went to see how Sheba was doing. She seemed glad to see me. Michael and Hank and Emily came, too.

"Oh," said Emily, "she's beautiful. Is she all yours? I think Sheba's an absolutely lovely name. You ride her all by yourself?"

It amazed me that Emily could sound so cheerful.

"She's not all mine," I told her. "She's really Elizabeth's, but Elizabeth doesn't ride her anymore. Henry says I should take her because she needs the exercise."

Just then Matthew came out of the privy. "Poor little orphans never seen a horse?" he taunted.

"Leave 'em alone, Matt," said one of the big boys, trying to steer him away. But Matthew just kept on pushing.

"Ignore him," said Hank.

"Nobody rides horses to school anymore, you know," Matthew went on. "Everybody rides bicycles. You will all have to go steal yourselves some. Wouldn't help, though. You ain't got no pa to teach you how to ride." He laughed.

Hank looked angry.

"Come on, Hank," Emily said. "Let's go back inside."

"Yeah, Hank," Matthew said, "just go back inside with the girls. You ain't got no pa to teach you to fight, either."

Suddenly Hank went flying at Matthew as if he was going to kill him. Everybody crowded around to see the fight. By the time Mr. Givens got out there to break it up, Matthew had a bloody nose and was hollering like a baby.

"Why don't you go home to that pa you're always bragging on," Hank said, wiping blood from his lip on his sleeve. "Maybe he can teach you some manners."

"You'll both be going home," Mr. Givens said, taking them each by the collar. "And you'll be taking a note from me with you."

Hank looked frightened at that. As Mr. Givens marched the boys off, Emily said, "Hank's afraid what the father will do. Peter ran away, and they blame

Hank for it. They said since he couldn't keep his brother here, he'll have to make up for it and do Peter's work, too. Hank doesn't say so, but the father hits him. He must be wondering what they'll say about him fighting at school."

With Matthew gone, the rest of the day was fairly quiet. Mr. Givens forgot about Matthew's toe in the excitement of the fight, so I didn't have to take a note home.

I was surprised to see Henry waiting when school let out. "How'd it go?" he asked.

"Okay."

"Must have been nice, being with others your age."

"Sure," I said, swinging up onto Sheba's back. I did not tell him about Matthew, or the fight, or standing in the corner. I did not tell him that I never wanted to go back.

As we were starting away, Emily came running over. A small boy was tugging on her arm.

"Hello, Mr. Jansen. Remember me? I'm Emily—I mean, Maryann. Hattie's friend from the home. I think she's so lucky to have gotten you. I mean lucky you chose her. I'd just love to be the only one. I can't imagine."

Henry shook his head. "You're a talker, ain't you?"

"That's what the mother says. I mean, Mrs. Dewhurst. That I talk too much. It makes her cranky."

Henry looked at Emily for a minute. "She'd be cranky anyway," he said. "You just keep talking, Emily. So she don't forget who you are."

Emily smiled up at him. Her eyes shone with tears. Then she turned and skipped off toward town, the boy dragging along behind her.

Henry watched her go and shook his head. "Ain't right, girl like that, so much life in her, placed out with the likes of that woman." He shook his head again, and I found myself wondering again if he was sorry he chose me instead of Emily. Emily would never have ended up in the corner on her first day of school. In all the time I'd known her, I'd never seen her angry.

13

On the ride back to the farm, I thought about writing to Mr. Bell. I would tell him about Emily and Hank. I would tell him to come and take us back. Even life at the home was better than this. At least there we fit in. Emily could have her name back, and Hank wouldn't have to worry about the father beating him.

I put Sheba in the barn, and fed and watered her. Then I went inside to help with supper. Henry was acting kind of peculiar, as if he didn't want me around. "Why don't you get on up to your room," he said. "You must have some schoolwork to do."

I tried to tell him that I didn't have much, but he wouldn't hear it. Perplexed and hurt, I went upstairs, hoping that Cloud would be there, happy to see me.

When I opened my bedroom door, my mouth fell open in surprise. The oak secretary from the attic stood by the window, freshly polished and smelling of lemon oil.

"To do your schoolwork at," said Henry, who had snuck up the stairs after me and seemed very pleased with himself.

I opened the desk and looked at all the little drawers and dividers. Henry had already stocked it with paper and envelopes. A brass inkwell and a gold-tipped pen sat on the desktop. And Henry had put some of my favorite books on the shelves above the desk. I ran my hand over the rich, golden wood. It was smooth and cool. "Elizabeth won't mind?" I asked.

"Don't fret about that," Henry said. "Better it be used than sit in the attic for the mice to build nests in."

Cloud seemed put out that our room had been changed. But when I sat down, she jumped into my lap and soon was purring away.

"Cat missed you," Henry said.

I smiled and scratched Cloud behind her ear. "Silly old cat," I said.

Henry smiled, too. "Supper's almost ready," he said. Then he turned and went downstairs.

I looked at the sheaf of white paper stacked neatly in the desk and thought about the letter I had planned

to write to Mr. Bell. "Oh, Cloud," I said, "it's all so con-
fusing. Sometimes I feel as though nobody wants me.
And then Henry does this."

Cloud looked at me with her big green eyes and
blinked. "At least I have you," I said, holding her close.
"Emily and Hank don't even have that."

Hank wasn't in school the next day, or the next.
Matthew was there, mean as ever, so I knew Mr. Givens
hadn't told the boys to stay away.

Emily didn't seem well. For the first time since I'd
known her, she was quiet and withdrawn.

"Are you ill?" I asked her.

She shook her head. "I'm all right," she said. "It's the
mother. She wants me to stop going to school." Tears
welled up in her eyes.

I felt myself growing hot in the cheeks. "She can't
do that," I said. "She agreed."

Emily shrugged. "She says a girl doesn't need an ed-
ucation. Schooling is for boys, she says. A girl doesn't
need to know reading and ciphering."

"But she promised Mr. Bell," I argued.

Emily shrugged again. "She says they'll never know.
She says no one from the home is going to check up,
and she needs me to help with the babies."

When I told Henry about it that night, he stabbed

his pitchfork into the ground and looked off thoughtfully in the direction of town.

After that, Emily didn't come back to school. Hank showed up one day with a black eye he said he got from Matthew, but I didn't believe him. It was the father, I knew. He was beating him. Hank was too proud to say—or too frightened. I wondered how long it would be before he disappeared, too.

"They promised us a better life," I told Cloud that night as we huddled together in bed, trying to stay warm. "But look what's happening. And nobody cares."

Over the next weeks and days, I grew accustomed to Matthew's taunts. I worked hard at school, and some of the students came to accept me. Mr. Givens even seemed to like me. He often pointed to my work as an example of fine scholarship. That didn't sit well with some of the other students, who made my life miserable, but I worked hard at my studies nonetheless.

I began to learn what to expect from Elizabeth. She had good spells and bad spells, as Henry said. But, as time passed, it seemed there were more good than bad. On her good days she was up and dressed, and we ate biscuits and gravy and had pies for dessert. On her bad days she took the medicine in the bottles next to her bed, then lay there and stared out the window, and Henry and I made do for supper. We did not have dessert. But good days or bad, she was still removed and distant.

I finally learned to milk Josephine.

"I think you've gotten to know each other well enough by now," Henry said one day when I was out in the barn cleaning the horse stalls.

It was hard at first to get the milk to flow, and I got my toes stepped on more than once. But after a while, Josie and I came to an understanding. And Cloud couldn't believe her good fortune. She just had to stand there and meow to get a drink of fresh warm milk sent her way. Henry hadn't been so generous.

The days were getting shorter, and every morning when I woke there was frost painted in lacy patterns on the windowpanes. The chickens had all but stopped laying. Henry said they did that when the days got short. What eggs they did lay were saved for cooking, so we had oatmeal for breakfast. The ground was frozen, which kept the dust down. But it hadn't been cold enough to freeze the pond. It was dark when I got up in the mornings, and when I finished my chores after school. It was too dark and cold to ride out to the cabin, so I sat in the house with Cloud, and with Elizabeth if she was up to it, and read at the table by the stove or did my schoolwork at my desk. It was colder upstairs, but I wrapped a quilt around my shoulders, and Cloud curled up in my lap and kept me warm.

After supper I read to Elizabeth. Willa Cather had become one of my favorites. I had only to look out the window to imagine myself right in the midst of her stories about Nebraska. I wondered if Elizabeth saw herself in them. I thought as I read about the early years in Nebraska, when Henry was a boy and before, that I could understand Henry a little better. But Elizabeth remained a mystery.

The end of October came and went without much note on the farm. At school they spoke of hayrides and bonfires for Halloween, but Elizabeth wouldn't go, and we couldn't leave her alone so long. I had been eager to go, in the hope that Emily might be there. Mrs. Dewhurst never even brought her to church anymore. I had expected Pastor Schiller to do something about it, but as the weeks passed and she didn't return, I realized he would not. So on Halloween night, I went to bed early and read myself to sleep.

It was cold and gray most days as fall crept past. One day I'd just gotten home from school and was brushing down Sheba when a strange buggy pulled into the yard. It was Pastor Schiller, finally come to call.

Henry came out of the house, looking suspicious.

"I've been meaning to stop by," the pastor said, smiling. "Is Elizabeth up to visiting?"

"She's sleeping," Henry said.

Was she really, or was Henry just saying that? The pastor looked the slightest bit relieved, I thought.

"Mind if I come in?" he said.

Henry shrugged and turned back toward the house. Pastor Schiller followed him in, and I came up behind.

Henry looked nervously down the hall to Elizabeth's room. I imagined he was wondering whether she'd stay there quietly, or come storming out and order Pastor Schiller out of her house. I was wondering the same thing myself.

"How is school going, Hattie?" Pastor Schiller said, turning to me.

"Fine," I said, casting my gaze to the floor. I didn't particularly appreciate the minister's attention.

"I hear good reports from Mr. Givens."

He was fairly beaming, as though it were to his credit that I was a good student. I wanted to ask him what reports he heard about Emily and Hank, but I didn't. What good would it have done?

"Yes, sir," I said.

"That's good, that's good," he said.

I could tell he was beginning to feel awkward. He was used to being invited in for coffee and cake, or something, I was sure. But Henry was just standing there nervously.

"One of our members kindly brought some clothes," he said at last. "Perhaps you could look through them and pick what you want, Hattie."

I nodded and headed for the buggy, glad to be out of the house. I'd chosen a couple of winter dresses and a long woolen coat and leggings when I heard Elizabeth's raised voice in the kitchen. I couldn't make out her words, but it was clear that Pastor Schiller wasn't welcome in her home. What had he done to make Elizabeth hate him so?

Soon after, Pastor Schiller came scurrying out of the house and climbed into the buggy. His ears were red, and he looked shaken. Still, he took time to say good-bye before he drove off. "Keep working hard at your studies," he said. "You're a smart girl. You'll do well."

I nodded. "Thank you." I was holding tight to those clothes, although I could just imagine what Elizabeth would say about being beholden.

By the time I got inside, Elizabeth was back in bed. Henry was giving her her medicine, and she was sleeping before long. That night I didn't have to sit with her. She slept straight through to morning.

After that, Elizabeth stopped going with us to church.

14

ewa

oward the end of November, it snowed. When
I woke up in the morning, the air was still. Snow
had covered the gray-brown landscape like a white-
wash, and it was still falling. Drifts were piled high
against the barn. Downstairs, I could hear whistling.

I dressed quickly and hurried to the kitchen and the
warm stove. Henry stopped whistling when I came in.
"No school today," he said. "This storm looks like it'll
last." He was smiling. I didn't understand why a blizzard would make Henry so happy. Then I remembered
the cow pond, and Henry saying that a good winter
might break the drought.

We had a large breakfast of potatoes and bacon and
biscuits with honey, and Henry even fried us each an
egg. What a treat. I was washing dishes and wondering what I was going to do in the house all day when

Elizabeth came bustling out of her room. She had a kerchief on her head and an apron around her waist. "Thursday is Thanksgiving," she said. "We'll bake today."

Henry actually grinned. "Guess I'll leave you two women to your kitchen," he said. He put on his coat and hat and headed out to the barn, whistling all the way.

The stove crackled in the silence he left behind him.

Elizabeth handed me an apron. "Best get to work," she said.

We brought two orange pumpkins up from the root cellar. Elizabeth gave me a knife and took one herself and started to cut up the pumpkin. I watched and tried to do the same, but my hands couldn't seem to follow hers. She worked with sureness and ease.

When she was done scraping out the seeds and cutting the pumpkin into chunks, she looked at me. "Lord, child," she said, throwing up her hands. "That's a pumpkin, not a piece of wood for whittling." Then she did something that surprised me. She smiled. I was so caught off guard, that smile seemed to go right into my heart, and I found myself laughing out loud. The poor pumpkin did look pitiful, all scraped and bruised.

"Sometimes I forget you haven't had a mama to teach you," she said, almost to herself. She took my pumpkin and showed me how to cut it open. Together we scooped out the seeds. "We'll get to them later," she said. And we each cut up half of the pumpkin and put it in the pot to boil.

While the pumpkin was boiling, we separated the seeds from the pulp and spread them on a baking sheet with some fat and salt. Elizabeth put the seeds in the oven to roast.

"What do you do with them?" I asked.

Elizabeth laughed. "Why, eat them, of course."

I couldn't imagine eating pumpkin seeds.

"You needn't make such a face," she said. Then we laughed together.

Elizabeth picked up my knife. "You do know how to peel apples, don't you?"

I looked at her smiling eyes and thought how pretty she was. I smiled back and reached for the knife. When I took it, our hands touched. Hers was warm and soft. I felt a lump at the back of my throat, as if a piece of apple were stuck there. I swallowed hard and turned away so she wouldn't see the tears that were stinging my eyes.

When Henry came in for lunch, there were pumpkin pies on the counter and apple pies in the oven. There was bread rising on the shelf over the stove.

"What, no pumpkin seeds left?" he said, looking around the kitchen.

I grinned and licked my fingers as I popped the last of them into my mouth. The salty goodness of it made my mouth water.

"Well," he said, "at least I can have one of those pies."

"I'm afraid not," said Elizabeth. "But there's a cold meat sandwich for you and there's coffee on the stove."

"A man works all morning in a blizzard and all he gets is a cold meat sandwich? Well, I never." Henry winked at me. "And not even a pumpkin seed."

I had never seen Henry and Elizabeth so cheerful. And I couldn't remember the last time I had felt so cheerful myself. Even with a blizzard raging outside, the kitchen was warm and cozy. I wished it would snow forever.

15

$\wp$

I might as well do some desk work," Henry said after lunch. "Not much sense in going out in this again." He looked out the window at the snow, which was still falling thickly. Then he sat down at his desk in the sitting room and went to work filling his pen with ink. He smoothed a clean piece of writing paper on his desk and began to write.

In the sitting room there was a fire in the fireplace. I sat in a rocker near the warmth, and Cloud settled in my lap, purring. Elizabeth put the bread in the oven. Then she came in and sat down opposite me with a basket of fine linen yarn, as white as the fresh-falling snow.

She lifted a crocheted tablecloth out of the basket. It was missing several squares. "I'd meant to finish this before the holidays," she said. A sudden sadness filled her eyes. Then she shook her head slightly, and her face took on a businesslike air. "Perhaps I can still get it done by Christmas if I work steadily."

She looked at me. "Are you handy with a needle?"

"Passable," I said. All the girls at the home were taught needlework so they would have a useful trade.

"Well then, you can work on these." She took a pile of linen napkins out of the basket. Each was embroidered in one corner with flowers in pastel colors. There was crocheted lace around the edges, and in the upper corners of two, names were stitched. "Henry" was stitched in blue on one. On another, in yellow, was the name "James."

Elizabeth saw me looking at it. "That was our boy," she said. She blinked as though holding back tears.

I realized then that I had never heard his name. "It's a handsome name," I said.

She nodded. "He was a handsome boy. Didn't even start one for my baby. She was gone before . . ."

I waited for her to say more. When she didn't, I asked, "What do you want me to do with these?"

"The lace is only basted on," she said. "It needs stitching."

I nodded. I could do that. I threaded the needle and began.

As I sewed, I looked up every so often to watch Elizabeth's fingers work that crochet hook. A white rosette formed in what seemed no time, then another and another. She stopped only to get the bread out of the oven. It smelled delicious. I struggled along, stitching the lace to the napkin edges. My fingers did not move quickly. Often I pricked them. But my stitches were straight and small. By the time Elizabeth had finished three rosettes, I had sewn all the way around James's napkin.

I held it out for Elizabeth to examine. She took it and ran her fingers over the name in the corner. "Fine work for a girl your age," she said. She put the napkin in her lap and picked up the crochet hook. I rethreaded my needle and started on Henry's napkin.

After a while, Elizabeth said, "I suppose you think it's foolish, keeping his napkin." Her fingers were still for a moment, stopped in mid-stitch. "This was his favorite time of year. Mine, too. He loved to help me roll out the dough for the pies . . ." She reminded me of Emily, the way she went on, as though if she kept on talking, she wouldn't have to think about anything. It had never occurred to me before that maybe that was why Emily talked so much.

Elizabeth paused for a moment. Then her fingers

85

began working again. "Do you miss your mama?" she asked.

My breath caught, and I pricked my finger. A small drop of blood formed on my fingertip. I sucked it off before it could get on the napkin.

I did not know what to say. My mama. What had she looked like? I knew she had black hair, like mine. And brown eyes. Elizabeth was staring at me. She expected an answer. I said, "They died when I was six. I don't remember much."

"My boy, James, was six," she said. "I miss him horribly."

"He had measles," I said. "Henry told me."

Elizabeth nodded. "But it was the pneumonia that took him." She paused. "They told me . . . Pastor Schiller said if I prayed . . . He said God would spare him. Then when he died, he said I should be grateful. Grateful that God had taken him so young." She turned her head and gazed out the window at the snow still falling. "I can't forgive him for that," she said scornfully.

She stopped and looked at me, as though I should say something. But I didn't. With death, I knew, words didn't help. And sometimes they even made it worse.

Now I knew why Elizabeth had been so angry when

the pastor came to call. Perhaps she and I had more in common than I had imagined. I looked down at Cloud, curled up in my lap in a warm gray ball. The end of her tail flicked as she slept. Cats, at least, never had to be grateful.

16

It snowed for three days. Henry whistled during each of them, and Elizabeth was up and preparing. It was hard not to be caught up in the excitement as we bustled about the kitchen.

On Thanksgiving Eve, I went to my room early. I sat at my desk and looked out the window into the darkness. Snow was swirling against the window. In the glass I could see my reflection. It was not the same dirty, frightened face that had stared back at me from the kitchen mirror when I first arrived. Now, I thought, it was time to write to Mr. Bell.

Dear Mr. Bell,

I am writing this letter to let you know that I am well here in Nebraska. I have been going to school and to church, as we agreed. The Jansens are good people, and we are beginning to feel that we belong together, I think.

Mrs. Jansen was ill when I arrived, but is much better now. I think maybe having me here has helped her.

I am sorry to report that not all of the children who were placed out here are doing so well. Peter has run away, as you may have heard, and Hank is beaten by the father. Emily can no longer go to school or to church, and is treated very poorly.

You asked me to write if I needed anything, and I do. Please help Emily and Hank.

I put down my pen and read my letter over. Satisfied with my work, I dipped my pen once more and signed it, "Gratefully yours, Hattie."

The next day I put the letter in my pocket before going downstairs. Elizabeth and I hurried about, packing up food. There were two pumpkin pies and two apple pies and three loaves of pure white bread. There were sweet pickles made from watermelon rinds, and dill and bread-and-butter pickles besides, brought up from the canning closet. I couldn't imagine who would eat it all.

It was Thanksgiving, and we were going to Henry's

mother's house in the city for the day. There was tension in Elizabeth's manner, and I wondered if she would be all right so far from home.

"An hour-and-a-half ride by sleigh," Henry said. "Be back by nightfall if the weather holds." He looked at Elizabeth with a nervous glance, and I saw that he was worried about her, too.

"Who will be there?" I asked Henry.

"Just family," he said.

Family. Did that include me? I remembered what Henry had said that first week, about Elizabeth not getting along with his family ever since James died. Maybe she was hoping this Thanksgiving would be a new beginning. She had been working awfully hard to prepare, these last few days. I'd never seen her so full of energy.

Henry brought the sleigh around, and he and Elizabeth packed it up. I thought Cloud could tell we were going to be gone for a while. She was pacing back and forth, rubbing against my leg. I picked her up and sat in the chair by the stove. "It's all right, Cloud," I said. "We'll be home tonight."

Henry came in. "Best leave the cat outside while we're gone," he said.

"But it's cold," I protested. Cloud snuggled deeper in my lap, as though she knew what Henry was saying.

"Can't leave her inside all day," he said. "She'll be fine in the barn. Jed and Old Moses will keep her company. And there's plenty of mice for her to eat."

I carried her out to the barn and brought her a bowl of milk. I gave her a hug, and she watched with sad eyes as I walked back to the house. I felt terrible.

Henry was at his desk. "Almost forgot that letter I wrote the other day," he said. "Haven't been able to get to town to mail it. Thought maybe somebody could do it for me in Lincoln." As he picked it up, I noticed the address. It was to Mr. Bell at the home. Henry must have seen me looking because he added, "He said to write if there were problems. Well, there are some, and I think he should know."

I was too stunned to say anything, but I suddenly felt sick to my stomach. I closed my hand tightly around the letter in my pocket. I had hoped to give it to Henry to mail for me. I had thought things were going well, that we were becoming a family. Elizabeth was getting better. But maybe that was it. Maybe now that Elizabeth was better, Henry thought she didn't need me anymore. It was all I could do to keep from crying as I walked out to the sleigh.

"Hop in," Henry said. "If we don't get going, it'll be time to head back before we even get there."

I climbed into the back and bundled myself up in

blankets against the wind. Henry gave the reins a flick, and we started off.

Whiteness spread around us like a blank page. The barbed-wire fences were covered in puffy ridges of white, as if painted with glue and sprinkled with goose down. Now and then a bird dotted the snowy landscape, searching out seeds and berries. It looked like a cold and lonely business, being a bird in Nebraska in winter. Henry chatted continually as we drove along. He'd become quite talkative lately. I'd come to take it as a good sign, and even enjoyed listening to his descriptions of Nebraska's natural wonders. But not today. Today I wasn't listening. I kept thinking about that letter. What had I done wrong?

My fingers and nose were numb and my toes ached by the time we reached Henry's mother's house. It was large and made of brick, and a snowman stood guard in the yard, with a broom for a musket. Once the house had stood alone, Henry said. But the town had grown around it. His papa had given up farming and sold the land for houses. Now the house was at the end of a tree-lined street full of other houses. I hadn't seen so many trees since I got to Nebraska.

Henry's mother was expecting us. "Oh!" she cried when she opened the door. "You must be Hattie. Such a skinny thing you are. It's good I made a big dinner."

She was a plump, gray-haired woman with a thick accent. Her long, thin hair was braided and wound tightly into a bun at the back of her head. It reminded me of the cinnamon rolls I saw in the bakery window in town.

"Come," she said. "You must be frozen. Take off your coat and warm yourself by the fire."

She reached out and took me by the hand. Her hand felt warm and soft and floury, like bread dough rising.

As she led me to the parlor, she said, "You must call me Grandmother. Everybody calls me that." She smiled and patted my hand. "Oh, so cold, those fingers."

Henry and Elizabeth were already in the parlor greeting the rest of the family. Everyone was laughing and smiling. Elizabeth's face was pale despite the long cold ride, and her smile looked forced. But I was too miserable myself to worry about her.

When I walked in, they stopped and stared. Grandmother said, "This is Hattie. Henry and Elizabeth's girl." I looked around at the faces. They all had sympathetic smiles. The poor little orphan, I could feel them thinking. I looked down at my feet. My floppy old shoes were even more worn than when I got them. I felt shabby and awkward. Henry and Elizabeth's girl, she called me—as though I were the servant.

17

Just then I heard a door slam in the hallway. Several children came barging into the parlor and stopped short. "Hey, look," yelled a boy, pointing his mittened finger at me. "It's the orphan."

"Thomas!" said Grandmother sternly, frowning at him over her glasses. "Say hello to Hattie."

Henry crossed the room and swooped the boy up onto his broad shoulder. "How's my favorite nephew?" he cried heartily. He carried the laughing boy out to the kitchen. "That your snowman I saw on my way in?"

"Those two," Grandmother said, shaking her head. "They're like father and son."

I could feel Elizabeth stiffen next to me. Grandmother must have felt it, too, because she looked embarrassed. No wonder Elizabeth hated it here.

Grandmother saw Elizabeth's cold gaze. She turned

to me awkwardly. "Well, Hattie," she said, "why don't you come in the kitchen with me? We can get acquainted while we finish the preparations."

It was my turn to stiffen. She *did* think I was the servant girl come to help out in the kitchen.

I looked at Elizabeth, who nodded her head firmly in Grandmother's direction. Apparently I had no choice but to follow. My cheeks burned as I was led out to the kitchen. Through the window I could see Henry playing in the snow with the boy called Thomas. He was smiling and laughing and throwing snowballs. Maybe if I'd been a boy he wouldn't have written to Mr. Bell, I thought. Maybe then he would have wanted to keep me.

"You know," Grandmother was saying, "we are alike, you and I."

I looked at her, unbelieving.

"It's true," she said. "I left my home in the old country when I was not much older than you. I came to America to make a better life, and I never saw my family again. I was like an orphan. I came to a new family in Nebraska. I didn't know them. They took me in. I worked for them—was their girl. Like you and my Henry and his Elizabeth."

I didn't say anything. I didn't tell her that leaving your family isn't the same as losing it; that I didn't come to Nebraska to be a paid servant girl. I looked out the window again. Henry had his arm around Thomas. His back was to me.

Thomas saw me looking. He stuck out his tongue. He wants me to know this is his family, I thought. He wants me to know I don't belong.

"You know what I always liked?" Grandmother was saying. "When I was in the kitchen, I got to taste the cookies before anybody else." She smiled like a guilty child and took a cookie off a plate on the counter. She handed it to me. "And there's no one to say, 'You're going to spoil your supper.' Here. Have one. They're my special recipe."

I took the cookie and ate a small bit. It was delicious: sweet and flaky. It melted on my tongue like butter.

"You like it, eh?" Grandmother grinned widely. "We're going to put some meat on you yet." She chuckled. "Now come on," she said. "We've got some work to do if we're going to get this supper on the table."

I had never seen so much food. There was a turkey almost as big as I was, and ham and roast beef. There were mashed potatoes whipped into a white mountain, squash with molasses drizzled on top, onions swimming in hot cream sauce, and green beans dripping with butter. Elizabeth's pickles were spooned into fancy glass dishes, and our bread was cut in thick slices and arranged on china plates.

The dining room table was bigger even than the ones at the home and laid out with a bright white cloth of linen, woven with shimmering flowers. Each place sparkled with china, silver, and glass. A second, smaller table was set for the children. But even the thought of all that food didn't stop me from dreading sitting with that horrid Thomas. What was there about him that Henry liked?

18

By the time Henry and the children came in from outdoors, it was snowing again. "Hope this lets up before it's time to go," Henry said.

"Never mind," said Grandmother, shooing him out of her kitchen. "Go dry off by the fire. Dinner is nearly ready."

"You, Hattie," she said, "you serve the children at the small table." She looked around at the jumble of food and dishes. "It's good to have help," she said. "I'm an old woman. I can't do what I used to do."

My cheeks burned. It wasn't that I minded serving. At Henry and Elizabeth's I worked all the time. But what about all those other children. Why didn't she ask them to help, too? I thought about Emily and wondered what Thanksgiving was like for her.

Henry's older brother, Sam, sat at the head of the large table. His wife, Martha, was next to him. Grandmother sat at the opposite end, with Henry and Elizabeth, and Henry's younger sister, Claire, and her husband, Frederick, in between. John, Henry's bachelor brother, sat next to Grandmother.

When everyone was arranged around the table, Sam stood up. "Heavenly Father," he began, "we thank You for all the blessings You have bestowed upon us, for the presence of loved ones, and for the feast You have placed before us on this Thanksgiving Day. We pray that You hold in Your loving care those who are not with us today, particularly little James, whom in Your infinite wisdom You saw fit to call home to You. We pray that You will help us to understand and accept those paths You have chosen for us. Also, today we welcome into our midst Hattie, the little orphan girl whom You have brought to us that she may be saved from a life of sin and destitution. Please help us to be patient and guide her along the path to salvation. For all of this, we are truly grateful. Amen."

By the time he was done, Elizabeth looked pretty angry. I knew I was. Henry looked nervous, as though he was afraid of what Elizabeth might do. But she just sat there, quiet, and ate.

Besides Peter and me, there were five other children at the small table: four little boys and a girl who looked about six years old. She was wearing a pale yellow dress and had white satin ribbons in her curly blond hair. Her shiny black shoes fit just right.

I shuffled my own worn shoes under the table. "What's your name?" I asked her.

"Mary Margaret," she said. Then she looked hard at me. "Why did Papa say you need saving?" she asked. "You a sinner?"

"Not a sinner," I said. "An orphan. Although some people seem to think they're one and the same."

Mary Margaret blinked, shrugged, then turned her attention to the mounds of food on her plate. I wondered if she knew how lucky she was to have a papa. I wondered what my own papa would have said if he'd heard that talk about me needing to be saved. I thought hard, trying to remember what my papa looked like, sounded like. I could not.

"It's really coming down," Henry said, looking out the window. The snow was so thick that you could not see through it.

"Will we be able to leave?" Elizabeth asked. She must have realized how eager she sounded. She looked embarrassed and added, "I mean, the animals. They'll need us."

I thought of Cloud at home in the barn. She would be waiting for me to come back and let her in out of the cold. Remembering Henry's letter, I thought that Cloud, at least, would miss me when I was sent away.

19

Supper was done and the dishes washed, and the snow was still coming down. Henry went out to check on the horses and give them some feed. When he came back, he looked glum.

"Guess we'll be bedding down here tonight," he said, rubbing Thomas's head.

"Hooray!" Thomas shouted, leaping into the air and running off to tell the other children. "Uncle Henry's staying!" I heard him hollering down the hallway.

Elizabeth looked anxiously at Henry. "You're sure there's no way to get home?"

Henry frowned. "It won't be the end of the world." He sounded cross.

"But the animals—" Elizabeth began.

"There's nothing I can do," Henry barked back. "Look out the window. We'd freeze."

Again I thought about Cloud, cold and alone in the barn. I'd promised her we'd be home tonight. She was depending on me.

Elizabeth looked at her hands. She fidgeted with the gold wedding band on her finger. I had a feeling it wasn't the animals so much as herself she was thinking about. And I didn't blame her. I wasn't eager to stay in that house overnight, with everybody thinking I was one step from the devil's front door.

Henry looked at Elizabeth a moment, then turned and walked out of the room.

"Well, I'm going to have a house full tonight." Grandmother's arms were full of bed linens and quilts. "Hattie, you'll have to help me make up the beds for all the little ones. I think some of you will have to share. But you won't mind that, will you?"

No, I thought, we orphans are used to sharing beds. But, to Grandmother, I just shook my head and took the armload of linens that she handed me.

I left Elizabeth alone in the sitting room, looking small and frightened. Everyone else seems to fit in here, I thought. Everyone but me and Elizabeth.

Upstairs the other children were running about, getting into their nightclothes and washing their faces. Grandmother had a real indoor bath and toilet. There would be no going out in the snow to the privy anyway.

"Hattie," Grandmother said, "you can take that room, and I'll take this. I guess we can put three of the boys in one bed and two in the other. You and Mary Margaret can share the bed in the other room, all right?"

I nodded, and she left me there with my arms full of linens.

Just then Thomas ran by with one of the other boys. "Look at the orphan," he said, sniggering. "She looks like a chambermaid."

Well, I don't care, I thought, my cheeks reddening. At least I don't have to share a room with that dumb Thomas.

It turned out that Mary Margaret was nearly as bad as Thomas. She had never shared a room before, let alone a bed. She wailed to her mama that she might catch bugs from that orphan.

"Now, Mary Margaret," her mama said, smiling, "I'm sure Hattie doesn't have bugs." She laughed as though she thought her daughter was the most adorable little thing.

I climbed into bed and closed my eyes. Mary Margaret complained that I had all the covers, and that she was freezing. "Mama," she called, "Hattie won't give me any quilts."

Her mama came in and patted her forehead. "We have to be generous," she told Mary Margaret. "Hattie didn't learn proper manners in that orphanage. It's our job to teach her."

I was so angry I could have spit. I threw the covers over on Mary Margaret and lay on my side of the bed, as close to the edge as I could without falling off.

Maybe it was just as well that I was going to be sent away. Then I wouldn't have to spend another Thanksgiving with Mary Margaret and the rest of Henry's hateful family.

It was cold, and even at the orphanage I had never felt so all alone in the world. I wished Henry or Elizabeth would come in to say good night and speak to Mary Margaret about the covers, but no one did.

Finally, I fell asleep. In the morning, I woke up shivering. Mary Margaret was lying under a mound of quilts, snoring, dead to the world.

I got out of bed and put on my stockings and shoes and went down to the kitchen. Henry was already outside, getting the horses ready to go. The snow had stopped; it was still dark.

Grandmother was at the stove, making breakfast. "Hungry?" she asked.

I shrugged. My stomach felt heavy, as if it were full of rocks.

"A good breakfast will keep you warm on the way home."

Home. Once, I had hoped Nebraska would be home. But no longer.

I looked at the heaps of food—potatoes, biscuits and honey, ham and sausages and even eggs. The very thought of eating made me feel sick.

Just then Elizabeth came down the stairs. She looked tired, and her eyes were red. From crying, I guessed. I wanted to cry, too, but couldn't somehow. So I looked at her and tried to smile encouragingly. It's almost over, I wanted to tell her; it will be all right. She at least could go home, but what would become of me?

I thought again about the letter still in my pocket. There was no point in posting it now. I would go back to the farm and wait for Mr. Bell to come for me. Would I be returned to the home, I wondered, or put on another train and made to start all over? My stomach ached at the thought.

20

After breakfast we bundled into the sleigh before anyone else was even awake. I noticed Henry hand his letter to Grandmother as he said goodbye. He said something I couldn't make out, and she looked at me and shook her head sadly. I looked away and tried to pretend that I didn't care what they were talking about.

The air was so cold that it hurt to breathe in. There was quiet all around, as though the whole world were asleep under a mountain of warm white quilts.

The animals heard us coming. They started to make all kinds of noise—whinnying and lowing and clucking and bleating. Henry jumped off the sleigh and headed straight for the barn. "You take care of the horses," he shouted to Elizabeth as he went. "Hattie, you come with me."

In the barn, Josie looked miserable. Her bag was swollen with milk. She was bellowing loudly. All the animals were calling for water and food. I looked around hurriedly for Cloud. I didn't see her anywhere.

"Cloud!" I called. "Where are you?"

"Don't worry about the cat now," Henry snapped. "We've more important things to take care of."

"But Cloud—" I started to argue.

"Hattie!" Henry was shouting. "Feed the chickens, then get to milking Josie. Now!"

"No!" I shouted back, hardly believing myself. "I've got to find Cloud."

I ran out of the barn to the back of the house, calling for her. But she was not there. The cabin, I thought. She must be at the cabin. I pulled my coat close around my neck to keep out the wind and started blindly to the back pasture. The snow was deep in places where it had drifted. Now and then I fell through above my knees. The wind blew snow off the ground into my face. It felt like needles pricking my skin.

"Cloud!" I cried. "Come here, Cloud. It's Hattie."

When I finally reached the cabin, my legs and face were numb with cold. I stumbled to the door and looked in, but Cloud was not there. I went back out into the wind. The pond was nearly clear of snow. The wind had blown it all into the grass. I walked over to the edge.

Across the pond was a small stand of apple trees. Perhaps Cloud was there, stuck in a tree or hurt. Henry had warned me to stay away from the pond, as the ice would be thin yet, and I might fall through.

"Cloud!" I cried again. Again, nothing but the wind answered back. I edged out slowly onto the ice. I was about to turn back when I saw a shadow under it.

At first I thought it was a patch of thin ice. Then I realized that the shadow had the shape of a small animal. A patch of gray fur was sticking through the ice. It was Cloud, drowned and frozen. Somehow she must have fallen through the ice and been unable to get out. The water had frozen around her, leaving her body suspended there.

I took off my glove and touched her fur with my finger. It was still soft. I put my face against it on the ice. My cheek burned with cold. Something inside me began to burn, too. I looked at Cloud's frozen form and remembered others I had lost—Mama, Papa, Georgie. It was a fire that had killed them, but they had seemed just as frozen in their coffins that day I had been taken to the funeral parlor to see their bodies, to say goodbye. But they hadn't looked real. They are only wax dolls, I'd thought. My real mama and papa will come and get me. Little Georgie will come to pester me. They will take me home and we will be together, just like always. But they hadn't. They had left me. All alone. With no one to love me. And I hated them.

I pounded the ice with my fists. "It's not fair! It's not fair!" I screamed. "I hate them all. Why did they leave me? It's not fair."

Suddenly the ice cracked open under me. The pond was shallow enough to stand in. I lifted Cloud's frozen body out of the water and carried her back to shore. I lay on the ground, cradling her in my arms as though she were a baby. As I lay in the snow, I felt that I was floating. It was quiet and restful. Half-awake, half-dreaming, I felt that I could finally sleep without waking, without dreams.

Then I heard a voice, felt someone lifting me. No! I wanted to shout. Don't wake me. Let me sleep. But I couldn't talk, couldn't move.

Later they told me they had found me in the snow, holding the frozen cat in my arms. Henry had ridden out to look for me after he'd finished with the milking.

They had feared I would die. My cheeks and hands were frozen. Elizabeth rubbed them with snow and spooned brandy into my mouth while Henry rode for the doctor.

It was Elizabeth's face I saw when I woke.

"Praise God," she said when she saw that I was awake.

I did not know her at first. I didn't know where I was. "Where's Mama?" I asked. "Where's Papa and Georgie?"

Elizabeth did not answer me. Then I remembered. Dead. All dead. And Cloud dead, too. "It's not fair," I said. Elizabeth shook her head. There were tears in her eyes. "No," she said. "It's not." She put her arms around me, and we cried together for a long time.

21

By the time the doctor arrived, my fingers and toes were aching.

"That's good," he said. "That means the blood is still circulating." He turned to Henry. "She's going to be all right."

"Thank God," Henry said.

I looked up at him, standing by the bed. There were tears in his eyes, too.

Elizabeth wouldn't let me get out of bed even though the doctor said I would be fine. "I'll not have you catching pneumonia," she said, so sternly it startled me. I knew she was thinking about James. She tucked the blankets in firmly around me. "You get some rest now," she said. She gently felt my forehead. Her touch was warm and soft. I looked at Henry. He winked at me and followed Elizabeth out to the kitchen. I could hear them talking, but I couldn't make out what they were saying.

I fell asleep then. I dreamed about Mama and Papa and Georgie, about a doll named Molly, about my singed black curls and scorched pink dress. I woke up screaming. Elizabeth came running in to see what was the matter.

"I had a dream," I said. "About the fire. There was smoke everywhere. I could hear Georgie calling, but I couldn't find him." I started to sob. "I was supposed to take care of him."

Elizabeth put her arms around me. "It's all right, child," she said. "You cry all you need."

The tears ran out at last. Elizabeth sat with me until I fell asleep again. All that afternoon I slept and dreamed, slept and dreamed.

At suppertime, Elizabeth brought me a bowl of hot broth, which I ate eagerly. It warmed me to my toes, which were still throbbing from the frostbite. Elizabeth sat on the bed while I ate, brushing the hair back from my face with her hand.

"You gave us such a fright," she said.

"I had to find Cloud," I said. "I shouldn't have left her. Henry shouldn't have—" I stopped. Of course Henry couldn't have known about the storm. He hadn't wanted to stay at Grandmother's, either. "She depended on me," I said finally. "I let her down. And now she's dead."

Tears welled in my eyes again. "Georgie depended on me, too," I said. "And Mama and Papa. And they are all dead. Why am I alive?"

"I know," said Elizabeth. "I feel the same way about James. And my little baby girl." She put her arms around me again, and I rested my head on her shoulder. She began to rock me back and forth gently, as if I were a baby.

We were both still crying when Henry came in. He stood by the bed for a moment with his hand on Elizabeth's shoulder. Then he said gently, "You go and finish the supper, Lizzie. I'll sit with Hattie for a while."

Elizabeth left, and Henry sat down next to me. "Feeling any better?" he asked.

"Yes," I said. "Some."

"I'm sorry about the cat," he said.

I sniffed. "It wasn't your fault."

"No, but I feel bad just the same."

"Henry," I asked him, "do you believe in God?"

"Yes, I do, Hattie. But not one who sits up in heaven deciding who should have good things happen to them, and who shouldn't. See, I also believe in luck, good and bad. When you had the courage to get on that train, you made your own luck."

Elizabeth came back into the room. "And ours," she said. "It was our good fortune Henry brought you home to us."

"But the letter," I said. "Didn't you write to Mr. Bell and tell him you didn't want me?"

Henry looked puzzled. Then he laughed. "Is that what you thought?" He put one arm around me. "That letter wasn't about you, child. It was about Emily and Hank. I told your Mr. Bell something had to be done about those children. It isn't right, them being treated so."

"So you weren't going to send me away?"

"Of course not, Hattie," Henry said. "Why, what would we do around here without you?"

"And you don't wish I was a boy?" I said, still a bit confused by all that had happened.

Henry looked surprised by that. "Whatever gave you that idea?"

I shrugged. It didn't matter. None of it mattered. I wasn't going to be sent away. I was home.

I lost track of time for a while, but I knew that more than one night had passed before I felt well enough to get out of bed and move to the sitting room. Elizabeth wrapped me in so many quilts, I thought I would suffocate. But there was no talking to her about it.

She sat and worked on her stitching and told me stories about her childhood, and about James. It was snowing again, and the fire was blazing in the fireplace. I was beginning to wonder where Henry was when I heard the kitchen door open and slam shut, and felt a blast of cold air that made me shiver.

Henry came in stomping his feet to get the snow off. Elizabeth jumped up to scold him about making puddles on the floor, but she stopped short. "Well now, what's this?" she said.

"Elizabeth," Henry said, gesturing grandly toward something I couldn't see from my seat by the fire, "you remember Emily, don't you? We saw her at church with Mrs. Dewhurst."

"Emily!" I wanted to jump up and run to her, but hadn't the strength. "Is it really you?"

"Oh, Hattie!" Emily cried, running in from the kitchen. "Oh, you look awful. Are you going to be all right? Henry told me about the accident, about the cat. I'm so sorry."

"Say, Emily." Henry interrupted her. "Are you going to tell them the news, or am I?"

Emily smiled. She actually looked at a loss for words.

"Well, somebody tell us," Elizabeth said.

"All right," Henry said, "I will." He drew up a chair and began unlacing his boots. "I went over to the Dewhursts' this morning, just as I said I would, Elizabeth. Wanted to see if I could borrow Emily for a bit, until you were well again, Hattie. Mrs. Dewhurst grumbled and insisted she couldn't possibly do without her."

"But then," broke in Emily, who was almost bursting with the news, "Mr. Jansen said how he'd written to Mr. Bell and told him how she'd not been letting me go to church and school and all, and Mrs. Dewhurst turned red as a beet, and then she told Mr. Jansen to keep me if he cared so much." Emily stopped and looked at Henry, and added, almost in a whisper, "And he said he would, thank you very much."

Henry was grinning ear to ear, and Emily's eyes were brimming with tears. Elizabeth clasped her hands together and shook her head in wonder.

I just smiled, and reached up to hug Emily. We were going to be a family, Elizabeth and Henry and Emily and I. And I was grateful. Truly grateful.

Jane Buchanan is a freelance writer who has been a newspaper reporter, photographer, and copy editor. Currently, she works at the public library in Meadville, Pennsylvania, where she lives with her husband and two teenage children.